D0382836

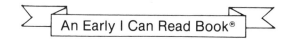An Early I Can Read Book®

WALPOLE

by Syd Hoff

HarperCollins*Publishers*

COLUSA COUNTY FREE LIBRARY

This book is a presentation of Newfield Publications, Inc. Newfield Publications offers book clubs for children from preschool through high school. For further information write to: **Newfield Publications, Inc.,** 4343 Equity Drive, Columbus, Ohio 43228.

Published by arrangement with HarperCollins Publishers. Newfield Publications is a federally registered trademark of Newfield Publications, Inc. I Can Read Book is a registered trademark of HarperCollins Publishers.

Walpole
Copyright © 1977 by Syd Hoff
All rights reserved. No part of this book may be used or reproduced in any manner whatsoever without written permission except in the case of brief quotations embodied in critical articles and reviews. Printed in the United States of America. For information address HarperCollins Publishers, 10 East 53rd Street, New York, N.Y. 10022.

Library of Congress Cataloging in Publication Data
Hoff, Sydney, date
    Walpole.

    (An Early I can read book)
    SUMMARY: Although Walpole is the biggest walrus in the herd, he would rather play with the baby walruses than be a leader.
    [1. Walruses–Fiction]   I. Title.
PZ7.H672Wam3   [E]   76-41514
ISBN 0-06-022543-2
ISBN 0-06-022544-0 lib. bdg.

For my granddaughter Shelli,
who will now want a walrus

Way up North

where it is always cold,

there lived a great herd of walruses.

The biggest was Walpole.

Walpole loved the cold.

Sometimes the walruses

pushed each other to get

the best place on the rocks.

6

But they never tried to push Walpole.

"It's time for you to lead the herd,"

said the oldest walrus.

"You are the biggest

and the strongest.

Polar bears never come near us

when they see your tusks."

"I don't want to be leader,"

said Walpole.

"I want to take care of

baby walruses

who have lost their mothers."

Walpole gave the little walruses

rides on his back

as if *he* were their mother.

10

He found food for them

on the ocean floor.

And he made sure they

did not float away

on a piece of ice.

The little walruses loved Walpole.

They barked like puppy dogs

when he walked on his flippers

and shook all over.

"Please be our leader,"

said the oldest walrus again.

"No," said Walpole. "I'm

having too much fun."

He dove into the water

to find food

for seven little walruses.

When Walpole came up,

he counted the walruses.

"One, two, three, four, five."

Two little walruses were missing!

"Where are they?" asked Walpole.

"They went that way,"

said the oldest walrus.

"They went that way,"

said another walrus.

"I better find them before

something happens to them,"

said Walpole.

Walpole swam away fast.

He swam to an island of seals.

"Have you seen any walruses?"

he asked.

"Sorry," said the seals.

"There's nobody here with

tusks and a mustache."

18

Walpole swam

until he came to a whale.

"Have you seen any walruses?"

he asked.

19

"Maybe I have.

Come in and see for yourself,"

said the whale.

And he opened his mouth wide.

Walpole swam away *very* fast.

He swam to an iceberg,

but there were no baby walruses

on one end of the iceberg,

and no baby walruses

on the other end of the iceberg.

There was only *ice*.

Then Walpole saw an Eskimo boy.

His boat was stuck in the ice.

"Can you get me out?" asked the boy.

Walpole hit the ice with his tusks.

He hit it again

and again and again.

The ice broke. The boat moved!

"Thank you for helping me,"

said the boy.

"You're welcome," said Walpole.

"Have you seen any little walruses?"

"No," said the boy. "But I

heard some barking on that iceberg."

25

Walpole swam as fast as he could.

And there were the little walruses!

They were so happy to see Walpole,

they barked and barked.

"Someday you will have a nice thick

coat of blubber like me," said Walpole,

"and you will never be cold."

Walpole swam back

with the two little walruses.

"Something seems wrong

with the herd," they said.

"Can you swim faster?"

27

Walpole swam very fast.

He got back to the herd

just as a huge polar bear

was chasing the oldest walrus.

Walpole roared.

When the polar bear

heard him roar

and saw his tusks,

he took off in a hurry.

"You came back

just in time to save us,"

said the other walruses.

"*Now* will you be our leader?"

asked the oldest walrus.

"Yes," said Walpole.

"If you still want me."

"We do," all the walruses roared.

And they never had to worry again.